ZB

THIS WALKER BOOK BELONGS TO:

_____

_____

_____

First published 1991 by Walker Books Ltd
87 Vauxhall Walk, London SE11 5HJ

This edition published 2008

2 4 6 8 10 9 7 5 3 1

© 1991 Nick Butterworth

The right of Nick Butterworth to be identified as
author/illustrator of this work has been asserted by him in accordance
with the Copyright, Designs and Patents Act 1988

This book has been typeset in New Century School Book

Printed in China

British Library Cataloguing in Publication Data:
a catalogue record for this book is available from the British Library

ISBN 978-1-4063-1243-0

www.walkerbooks.co.uk

My Grandma is WONDERFUL

Nick Butterworth

WALKER BOOKS
AND SUBSIDIARIES
LONDON • BOSTON • SYDNEY • AUCKLAND

My grandma is wonderful.

She always buys
the biggest ice-creams ...

and she never,
ever loses at noughts
and crosses …

and she knows
all about nature ...

and she's brilliant
at untying knots ...

and she's always
on your side when
things go wrong ...

and she makes
the most fantastic
clothes ...

and when you're ill,
she can make you forget
that you don't feel well ...

and she can scream
really loudly …

and she has
marvellous hearing ...

and no matter where
you are, she always
has what you need
in her handbag.

It's great to have a
grandma like mine.

She's wonderful!